Dragon Slayers' Academy™ 18

NEVER TRUST A TROLL!

By Kate McMullan
Illustrated by Bill Basso

GROSSET & DUNLAP

This one's for you, Dylan Brandt—K.M.

GROSSET & DUNLAP
Published by the Penguin Group
Penguin Group (USA) Inc., 375 Hudson Street, New York, New York 10014, U.S.A.
Penguin Group (Canada), 90 Eglinton Avenue East, Suite 700, Toronto, Ontario,
Canada M4P 2Y3 (a division of Pearson Penguin Canada Inc.)
Penguin Books Ltd, 80 Strand, London WC2R 0RL, England
Penguin Ireland, 25 St Stephen's Green, Dublin 2, Ireland
(a division of Penguin Books Ltd)
Penguin Group (Australia), 250 Camberwell Road, Camberwell,
Victoria 3124, Australia (a division of Pearson Australia Group Pty Ltd)
Penguin Books India Pvt Ltd, 11 Community Centre, Panchsheel Park,
New Delhi—110 017, India
Penguin Group (NZ), Cnr Airborne and Rosedale Roads, Albany,
Auckland 1310, New Zealand (a division of Pearson New Zealand Ltd)
Penguin Books (South Africa) (Pty) Ltd, 24 Sturdee Avenue, Rosebank,
Johannesburg 2196, South Africa

Penguin Books Ltd, Registered Offices:
80 Strand, London WC2R 0RL, England

Text copyright © 2006 by Kate McMullan. Illustrations copyright © 2006 by Bill
Basso. All rights reserved. Published by Grosset & Dunlap, a division of Penguin
Young Readers Group, 345 Hudson Street, New York, New York 10014. DRAGON
SLAYERS' ACADEMY and GROSSET & DUNLAP are trademarks of Penguin
Group (USA) Inc. Printed in the U.S.A.

Library of Congress Control Number: 2006021336

ISBN 0-448-44393-7   10 9 8 7 6 5 4 3 2 1

Chapter I

Summer vacation was over. Wiglaf of Pinwick was itching to get back to Dragon Slayers' Academy. That's why, on a blue-skied fall morning, he stood outside his family's hovel in his DSA uniform. All he owned was tied in a bundle at the end of a stick.

"Dudwin!" Wiglaf called. "Are you coming?"

Wiglaf's third-youngest brother darted outside with a pack on his back. "I can't wait to go to school!" he said.

Now Wiglaf's father, Fergus, and his mother, Molwena, and his eleven other brothers crowded together in the hovel doorway.

"Bye, Wig!" the brothers called. "Bye, Dud!"

As the two started off, Fergus called, "Knock, knock!"

Wiglaf rolled his eyes. His father told really, really bad knock-knock jokes.

He answered, "Who's there?"

"Howard!" cried Fergus.

"Howard who?" said Wiglaf.

"Howard you like some cabbage soup?" boomed Fergus.

Molwena bustled over. She thrust a flagon of warm cabbage soup into Wiglaf's hands.

"The hovel will seem empty without you lads," Molwena said. Then she twirled around three times and spat on the ground for good luck. "Wiggie, promise to keep an eye on your little brother."

"I promise, Mother," said Wiglaf.

At last, with more waving and good-byeing, the lads set off.

"I cannot wait to see Daisy again," said Wiglaf as they walked beside the Swamp River.

Thanks to a wizard's spell, Wiglaf's pig, Daisy, spoke Pig Latin. Wiglaf's mother did not want Daisy around, for she feared that a talking pig would bring bad luck. So Daisy had spent the last weeks of summer with Erica.

"Lucky Daisy," said Dudwin. "Staying at the Royal Palace. Oh, look, Wiggie. There's the message tree."

The lads stopped beside a gnarled old oak. Messages of all sorts hung from its branches:

Garth,
Get in touch with your mother right away!
Love,
Mother

Mother,
Backeth off!
Your son,
Garth

Dudwin pointed to a message with a drawing of a dragon.

"Wiggie!" he said. "Read this one."

Wiglaf read aloud:

BUBBLES ALERT!!!!!

The water dragon known as BUBBLES has been spotted in Leech Lake. Do not be fooled by his friendly blue eyes. Or his cheery smile. BUBBLES is dangerous—VERY dangerous.

Here is how ye shall know him:

Full name: *Bubbles von Troubles*

Mate: *Duckie McScales (slain by Sir Trom, the brave and bold)*

Appearance:

    Scales: *sea blue*

    Horn: *tenor sax*

    Eyes: *navy blue*

    Feet: *webbed*

Often heard saying: *"Surf's up!"*

Biggest surprise: *he's not a flamer*

Hobby: *water ballet*

Favorite thing in all the world: *playing "Blue Dragon" on his horn*

His mark: *B on a tree*
Secret weakness: *Ah-ah-ah-ah...*

"Ah-ah-ah-ah?" said Dudwin. "What does that mean? I don't think Bubbles sounds so scary."

"You never know with dragons, Dud," said Wiglaf. He opened the flask. They held their noses and gulped down most of their mother's cabbage soup. Then the lads walked on.

At last they reached the slimy waters of Nowhere Swamp. In the middle was a patch of quicksand known as Wizard's Bog. A row of rocks poked up, making a path across the swamp.

It was right here, a year ago, that Wiglaf first met Zelnoc. It was here that the wizard put a Pig Latin speech spell on Daisy. It was here that Zelnoc gave Wiglaf his magical sword, Surekill. Too bad the wizard had forgotten the magic words that would make the sword leap from Wiglaf's hand and slay a dragon.

"Be careful crossing, Dud," said Wiglaf. "The

quicksand is very quick."

"Oh, fie, Wiggie!" said Dudwin. "I've crossed this swamp a hundred times. Watch this!" He began hopping from rock to rock on one foot.

Wiggie's stomach knotted up as he watched. Why did Dudwin always have to show off?

"I'm almost across!" Dudwin shouted. Then he took a bad hop and splashed into the swamp.

Wiglaf raced across the rocks toward his brother.

"Wiggie, help!" cried Dudwin. "I'm sinking!"

"I'm coming, Dud!" cried Wiglaf. When he was close enough, Wiglaf stuck out the stick that held his bundle. "Grab on!" he cried.

Dudwin grabbed the end of the stick.

"Pull harder, Wiggie!" wailed Dudwin. "I'm going down fast!"

"I'm trying!" called Wiglaf, wobbling on a rock. He was half afraid he'd fall, too.

Then suddenly his brother began to rise out of the quicksand. Up, up, up! Wiglaf had a funny feeling that he wasn't the one pulling Dudwin up. How was it happening?

Dudwin let go of the stick. He kept rising.

"Look, Wiggie! No hands!" cried Dudwin.

Now Wiglaf saw a pair of scrawny arms under his brother, lifting him out of the swamp. The arms were followed by a pointed hat. The hat was followed by the face of an ancient wizard.

"Zelnoc!" exclaimed Wiglaf.

"That's my name, don't wear it out." The wizard continued to rise magically out of the swamp. From the tip of his hat to the soles of his slippers, Zelnoc was coated in swamp ooze. So was Dudwin. The wizard glided over and set Wiglaf's brother down on the bank.

"Thanks, wiz," said Dudwin. "That was awesome."

Zelnoc smiled. "What sort of gift would you like, lad?"

"I get a gift?" said Dudwin.

The wizard nodded. "Wizard Rule Number

886 says that if I save your life, I must give you a gift."

"You don't have to take it, Dud," said Wiglaf. Zelnoc's gifts could backfire in strange ways.

"Surely you jest!" said Dudwin. "I love gifts! Okay, wiz—do you have something that will turn me invisible?"

"No, Dud!" cried Wiglaf. "Zelnoc's spells—they always go wrong!"

"Hush, Wiglunk!" said Zelnoc. "I've been soaking in the power-restoring quicksand for three weeks. My magic is in tip-top shape."

The wizard extended his skinny swamp-oozy arms out in front of him and turned his palms up. He began to chant:

"Zippity-Zippity, Zoopity-Zoopity,
Zupity-Zupity, Zap!
Give this lad the Invisible Cap!"

A light flashed. ZAP! And Zelnoc was holding

a bright blue cap decorated with silver lightning bolts.

"Awesome!" said Dudwin.

"For you, lad," Zelnoc said, placing the cap on Dudwin's head.

"What do you think of my spells now, Waglip?" asked the wizard.

"Do you know the magic words to make it work?" Wiglaf asked.

"I certainly do," said the wizard huffily. "When you want to become invisible, lad, say, 'Zippity Zap.' And when you want to reappear, you say, 'Zappity Zip.' That's all there is to it."

"Zippity Zap!" said Dudwin.

Instantly, he vanished.

"Can you see me?" asked Dudwin's voice.

"No," said Wiglaf. "Reappear now, Dud."

"Zappity Zip!" said Dudwin.

And there he was again.

Wiglaf breathed a sigh of relief. It was amazing. Zelnoc's spell worked perfectly. Three weeks in the swamp really had done the trick.

"Thanks, wiz!" said Dudwin.

"Tah-tah, lads," said Zelnoc. "I'm off to see Zizmor. The Amazing One is still miffed at me for breaking his brand-new Cloud Maker. But now, with my powers restored, I can fix it!"

A blast of purple smoke rose around the wizard. When it vanished, the wizard had, too.

"Zounds, Wiggie!" exclaimed Dudwin. "This cap shall make me the envy of all the Class I lads and lasses!"

"Just be careful, Dud," said Wiglaf. "If you go showing it off at school, Mordred will take the cap away from you."

"That's not going to happen!" said Dudwin. Then he cried, "Zippity Zap!" and vanished.

Wiglaf leaped over the rocks after his invisible brother. He had a feeling that this cap would bring nothing but trouble. And how could he keep an eye on Dudwin if he couldn't even see him?

Chapter 2

Wiglaf and Dudwin, visible once more, ran over the drawbridge and through the gatehouse of Dragon Slayers' Academy.

Wiglaf smiled as he looked around the castle yard. It was filled with blue-uniformed students. And Class I lads and lasses, like Dudwin, who did not have their DSA tunics yet. The headmaster was holding a clipboard and collecting pennies from the Class I students. And there beside the scrubbing block was Sir Mort!

Wiglaf waved hello to the old knight. "How good it is to be back at school!" he said.

"I love it here already!" said Dudwin.

"Iggy-way!" cried Daisy. The pig galloped across the castle yard and sprang into Wiglaf's arms.

"Daisy!" cried Wiglaf, swaying under the weight of his dear pig. "How I have missed you, girl!" He put her down.

"E-may, oo-tay," said Daisy.

"How did you like living at the Royal Palace?" Wiglaf asked.

"Onderful-way," said Daisy. *"I-yay ook-tay a-yay ose-ray etal-pay ath-bay every-yay ay-day."*

"That's why you smell so sweet," said Wiglaf.

"You do smell good, Daisy," said Dudwin. "How do you like my new cap?"

"Ery-vay ice-nay," said Daisy.

"The wizard gave it to me," said Dudwin. "Watch this!"

"Dudwin," warned Wiglaf. "What did I tell you?"

"I just want to show Daisy," said Dudwin.

"Not now," said Wiglaf. "Not with everyone around."

Erica ran over to them.

"Wiggie!" she cried. "Can you believe we're in

Class II? I plan to run for class president. Can I count on your vote?"

"Sure," said Wiglaf.

Janice came bounding across the yard next. "Hey, Wiggie! Hey, Dudwin!" she said. "I'm so glad to be back!"

Wiglaf saw that Janice had tooth marks on her neck and arms. Her baby brother, Bibs, was clearly still in his biting stage.

"Have you heard? A dragon's in the neighborhood!" Janice clapped her hands together. "The excitement starts already!"

"What dragon?" asked Wiglaf. "Do you mean Bubbles? We saw a notice about him on the message tree near Pinwick."

"That's the one!" said Janice. "Bubbles is said to be a terrible monster. If he shows up, I shall run him through with my lance!"

Now Angus hurried over to greet them.

"Wiglaf!" he said. "I have saved you the cot next to mine in the Class II dorm."

"Thanks!" said Wiglaf.

Angus turned to Dudwin. "Go pay Mordred your eight pennies before he runs out of new DSA tunics, Dud," he said.

"Right!" said Dudwin, who had sold a dragon fang necklace he'd made at camp for exactly eight pennies.

"See you later, Wiggie!"

Wiglaf watched his brother join the other new students. One lad stood out from the bunch. He was a head taller than the others. His ears were pointed. And his skin was bright green.

"It looks like a troll lad is in Dud's class," said Wiglaf.

"He is," said Angus. "Trolls are big and strong, so Uncle Mordred thinks they'd make great dragon slayers. He put the word out that trolls are welcome at DSA."

As Wiglaf watched, the troll bent down and picked up a big nightcrawler worm from the ground. He dangled it over his mouth. The other new students reacted with a mix of horror and delight.

The troll let go of the worm and caught it on his pointy tongue. Then he closed his mouth and swallowed.

"Guh-huh, guh-huh, guh-huh!" laughed the troll.

"Oooh, gross!" cried some students.

Yet many others looked at the troll with admiration.

"What a show-off," said Angus.

"Maybe it's because he's the only troll here," said Wiglaf. Right then and there, he decided to become the troll's friend. He would tell Dudwin to be extra-friendly to him, too.

The lunch bell sounded. Moments later, Wiglaf and Angus were picking up trays in the dining hall.

"What'll it be?" asked Frypot. "Cream of eel-and-moat-weed soup? Chopped eel on a bun? Or the soup 'n' sandwich combo?"

It looked like the lunch menu hadn't improved over the summer.

"What do you recommend?" asked Angus.

"Made the soup week before last," Frypot said. "And the chopped eel smells funny." He shrugged and tossed the lads a few small parchment packets. "Whichever you take, douse it with red pepper sauce," he added. "Covers up the foul taste."

Wiglaf and Angus carried their trays across the dining hall.

"Oh, no," Angus wailed suddenly. "Look! At the Class I table! It's my horrible cousins, Bilge and Maggot!"

Wiglaf saw the twins. They had on brand-new DSA tunics. But their faces and hands were as filthy as ever. They were trying to start a food fight.

Dudwin wasn't sitting at the Class I table yet. Neither was the troll. Wiglaf spied him standing at the slit in the castle wall, looking outside. Maybe he was hoping to see other trolls on their way to DSA.

"How could Uncle Mordred let Bilge and Maggot into DSA?" wailed Angus as he took a seat at the Class II table.

"Good soup," said Erica, who liked everything about DSA. "What's wrong, Angus?"

"Bilge and Maggot are here. They are the worst lads in the world," Angus declared. "They shoved Uncle Mordred's wheelbarrows full of gold into the moat, remember?"

Erica nodded. "How could we forget?"

"Aha!" said Janice. "That explains why there's a Moat Diving class this fall."

A scream rang out in the dining hall.

"Ghost!" cried several Class I students.

Startled, Wiglaf looked around. Everyone was pointing at a cafeteria tray. It was floating mysteriously across the dining hall.

"Oh, no!" wailed Wiglaf. "I warned Dudwin not to show off!"

"Dudwin?" said Erica. "I don't see Dudwin."

"That's the problem," Wiglaf said. "Zelnoc gave him a magic cap that can turn him invisible."

Suddenly sparks began shooting all around the tray.

"Ow!" cried Dudwin's voice. "Ow! Stop!"

The tray clattered to the ground. As soup went flying, Headmaster Mordred jumped up from the head table.

"Blazing King Ken's britches!" he cried. "What vile spirit haunts my school?"

Dudwin did not answer, but the sparks kept flying. Suddenly, Dudwin's head appeared. Just as suddenly, it vanished. Now his arms appeared, and disappeared. One leg appeared, and stayed visible as other parts of Dudwin blinked on and off.

"Ow, ow, ow, ow!" cried Dudwin's voice.

"Fiend!" shouted Mordred. "Be gone!"

Wiglaf leaped up. "Say 'Zappity Zip,' Dud!" he shouted.

"Zip—ow! Zap!" Dudwin cried.

The next time Dudwin's head appeared, Wiglaf grabbed the cap and yanked it off.

"Yikes!" cried Dudwin, falling to the ground. The cap gave off a few more sparks and quit.

"Go ahead. Say 'I told you so,'" said Dudwin,

getting to his feet. "I shouldn't show off. I'm sorry."

"It's okay, Dud," said Wiglaf. "You put on a pretty good show."

Dudwin looked around the room. Everyone was staring at him.

"Thank you very much," said Dudwin, bowing from the waist. "The next show will be tonight after supper."

All the lads and lasses laughed.

But Mordred was not laughing.

"What is the meaning of this?" he boomed as he strode across the dining hall.

Wiglaf whisked the cap behind his back.

"My brother Dudwin meant no harm, sir," he said quickly.

Mordred scowled at Dudwin. "Don't I know you from someplace?" he asked.

"I went to your camp this summer, Mordie," said Dudwin.

"Mordie was for camp!" boomed Mordred. "Here at school, you'll call me sir! And we'll have no more of—whatever that was, eh?"

"Right, sir," said Dudwin.

Mordred stomped off.

"Give me my cap back, Wiggie," said Dudwin.

"I don't know, Dud," said Wiglaf.

"Please, Wiggie! It's mine!" said Dudwin.

Reluctantly, Wiglaf handed it to Dudwin, who ran to the trash barrel and threw in the cap.

"Good riddance, huh, Wiggie?" said Dudwin. Wiglaf smiled. Dudwin had been at school for only an hour, and already he was smarter.

By the time Wiglaf returned to the Class II table, his soup was cold. He was holding his nose and slurping some down when pounding footsteps sounded. A sweet scent filled the air. Wiglaf turned to see the troll running through the dining hall.

"Run fer yer lives!" the troll shouted. "Dragon outside! Terrible dragon!"

"A blue dragon?" yelled Erica.

"Yah!" shouted the troll.

"With a red horn on his head?" yelled Wiglaf.

"Yah!" shouted the troll.

"Is he swimming in the DSA moat?" yelled Janice.

"Yah!" shouted the troll.

"It's Bubbles!" cried everyone at the Class II table.

"To arms!" yelled Mordred. "Grab your swords, lads and lasses! Slay that dragon!"

"But we don't have swords!" cried a Class I lad.

"Then improvise!" cried Mordred. "Use whatever's handy."

All the lads and lasses leaped up. Many held spoons as they ran from the dining hall.

Wiglaf's heart pounded with fear. Bubbles was right outside in the DSA moat! Janice was right. School was starting off with a bang.

Chapter 3

As Wiglaf ran, he drew his rusty sword. He would never stab Bubbles. He hated the sight of blood. Yet waving Surekill made him feel brave.

All the future dragon slayers ran out to the castle yard. They streamed over the drawbridge.

"He's in the moat!" yelled the troll. And then he ran back toward school.

Erica stood at the foot of the drawbridge, giving orders.

"Go left!" she said to a group of Class I lasses waving sticks for their weapons. "Those of you with spoons, go right! We'll encircle the moat while Bubbles is underwater. When he comes up, he'll be surrounded."

Weapons aloft, the DSA students stood ready.

All eyes were on the moat. They waited for Bubbles to surface.

"Bubbles can hold his breath a very long time," Wiglaf said at last.

Angus peered down into the water. "All I see are eels. No dragon."

"Perhaps he is down in the deepest part," said Wiglaf.

"If a dragon were in the moat," said Angus, "wouldn't the eels be thrashing around?"

"You would think so," said Wiglaf.

"Bubbles!" called Erica, drawing her silvery sword, which was an exact replica of Sir Lancelot's. "Come up and meet your doom!"

Bubbles did not come.

"Bubbles!" called Janice, pounding her lance on the ground. "Are you a cowardly worm?"

Maybe he was, thought Wiglaf, for there was still no sign of any dragon.

Now Wiglaf heard a faint sound: "Guh-huh! Guh-huh! Guh-huh! Fooled you!"

He looked up. There at the slit in the castle wall stood the troll, laughing his head off.

"'Tis a trick!" cried Wiglaf. "Bubbles is not in the DSA moat. Look!"

Wiglaf saw Bilge and Maggot poke their heads out next to the troll. And Dudwin. He was there, too. All four lads were laughing.

"Fooled by Class I lads!" cried Janice. "What an insult!"

"'Tis indeed!" Erica said angrily. "Wiggy, Dudwin is falling in with a bad lot. You'd better teach your brother how to behave."

"'Twas a harmless prank," Wiglaf said lamely. Once classes began, the troll would probably calm down. He hoped Dudwin would, too.

That afternoon, Wiglaf put his thin blanket on the not-too-lumpy cot next to Angus's cot. He took out the few items from his bundle, and he was unpacked.

Wiglaf walked down the hall and peeked in the

doorway of the Class I lads' dorm.

Dudwin was sitting in a circle on the floor with Bilge, Maggot, and the troll. They were playing cards. Other Class I lads were watching.

"I won, didn't I?" the troll shouted. "Hand over yer pennies."

"But we don't have any pennies," said Bilge.

"Yeah," said Maggot. "Not a one."

"Ye have any pennies?" the troll asked Dudwin.

"I did," said Dudwin proudly. "But I gave them to Mordred."

"So, ye can't pay," said the troll. "That means ye owes me, understand?"

"Yeah," said Maggot and Bilge and Dudwin.

Wiglaf crept away from the door. What did the troll mean that they owed him? He didn't like the sound of it.

At the henhouse, Wiglaf found Daisy sitting in the straw, surrounded by softly clucking hens. She had her snout in a book: *Famous Pigs in History.*

"Hello, Daisy," said Wiglaf. "I see you have

already been up to the library."

"*Es-yay,*" said Daisy. "*Is-thay is-yay a-yay ood-gay ook-bay.*"

Daisy told Wiglaf about some famous pigs. Then Wiglaf told Daisy how the troll had tricked everyone by saying that the water dragon Bubbles was in the DSA moat.

"Dudwin looks up to the troll," said Wiglaf. "I can tell. I think if the troll told Dudwin to do something bad, Dudwin would do it."

"*On't-day orry-way, Iglaf-way,*" said Daisy. "*Udwin-day is-yay a-yay ood-gay ad-lay at-yay eart-hay.*"

Wiglaf smiled. Daisy's wise words made him feel better. Dudwin was a good lad at heart. And no doubt the troll was, too. Wiglaf was a worrywart, that was all.

"What'll it be for supper, lads?" Frypot asked Wiglaf and Angus. "Eel tail stew? Or the eel-and-moat-weed wrap?"

"What do you recommend?" asked Angus.

"Always safest to take the cooked dish," Frypot said.

Lady Lobelia stood up. She clinked on her water goblet just as Wiglaf and Angus took their places at the Class II table.

"Attention, lads and lasses!" Lady Lobelia said. "Welcome to a new school year at DSA. For those of you who don't know me, I am Lady Lobelia, Headmaster Mordred's sister. Mordred and I both have some important announcements."

Wiglaf happened to see the troll put his hand to his mouth and belch loudly.

Mordred jumped up. "Who burped?" he boomed.

The troll did not confess.

"We'll have no more of that," Mordred said. "If there's any belching to be done around here, I'll do it. Understood?"

In answer, the troll belched again.

Everyone at the Class I table cracked up laughing.

Mordred stared at the Class I students. His face turned purple with rage. "One more belch and I'll throw the whole lot of you into the dungeon." Mordred raised his bushy left eyebrow, making his left eye bulge scarily out of its socket. "And we'll have no more pranks like the one this afternoon."

"Class I?" said Lady Lobelia. "Please stand and tell us your name, where you're from, and why you are here at DSA."

Dudwin popped to his feet.

"Hi, everybody!" he said. "I'm Dudwin from Pinwick. I came here to go to school with my big brother Wiglaf. He has slain two dragons!"

Wiglaf smiled. Dudwin could be a pain. But he was a loyal brother.

"You're here because you want to become a dragon slayer, too. Aren't you, lad?" asked Mordred.

"Maybe," said Dudwin. "Maybe not." He sat down.

Bilge and Maggot stood up next.

"I'm Bilge!" shouted Bilge. "That's Maggot!"

"We live in a cave and eat raw bugs and worms!" shouted Maggot.

"Ewwww!" cried some students.

"Aw right!" cried the troll, pumping a great green fist in the air.

Mordred groaned. "What I do for my family," he muttered. "Sit down, you clowns!" he boomed. "Next!"

A lass stood up now. "I'm Agatha. Call me Aggie. I'm from Toenail."

"Hooray for Toenail!" cried Torblad from the Class II table.

"I'm here because I hear the food is totally great," said Aggie.

Frypot stuck his head out of the kitchen. "Really?" he asked.

"Nah!" said Aggie. "Gotcha!" And she doubled over, laughing.

"What a bunch!" mumbled Mordred. Then he

said, "And do you wish to become a dragon slayer, Aggie of Toenail?"

"Not really," said Aggie. "But I need something to fall back on in case my singing career doesn't work out."

Mordred glared at her and bellowed, "Next!"

Now the troll rose. Wiglaf looked at his bare feet. Each foot had one big toe and seven smaller toes.

"Grock is me name," the troll said. "I lives under the Killerfish River Bridge with me family. Sometimes humans drives their wagons over the bridge and me family robs 'em. That's how I got me eight pennies to come here to school."

The troll grinned, showing a mouth full of big, crooked teeth.

"Other times humans steers their boats under the bridge," the troll went on. "And me family robs 'em, too. Or, if we feels like it, we eats 'em." Grock licked his lips.

A worried murmur swept the dining hall.

"I won't eat anyone here," said Grock. "Promise!" He grinned again.

"And why have you come to DSA, Grock?" asked Mordred.

"Don't want to go into me family business, do I?" said Grock. "Want to become first troll dragon slayer!"

"Excellent!" Mordred grinned at Grock. "Welcome, troll lad!"

Now Lobelia stood up again. "Each of you Class I lads and lasses will have a buddy from Class II. You will spend the first week of school with your buddy, who will explain all about DSA."

"Hope I get Dudwin," Janice said.

Wiglaf hoped he would get Grock as his buddy. He knew he could help the troll get used to DSA.

"Class I, push your table and benches over to the wall," Lady Lobelia said.

Grock picked up the Class I table and threw it against the wall.

"Whoops!" he said. "Sometimes I forgets me own strength."

Lobelia rolled her eyes. "Make a circle in the middle of the dining hall," she said.

Class I did as they were told.

"Class II," said Lady Lobelia, "form a circle outside theirs. Everybody hold hands."

Wiglaf stood in the big circle between Janice and Erica.

Coach Plungett stood up with his mandolin. "Just listen to the song, and you can't go wrong," he said. "Class I, circle to the right. Class II, circle left."

Wiglaf and the others in Class II began moving to the left.

"Close your eyes. When I stop singing, freeze." Coach began to play his mandolin and sing:

"Everybody needs a buddy,
A buddy wise and true!
When you're new and need some help,

Your buddy's there for you!"

Everybody kept circling while Coach sang verse after verse of the buddy song. At last he sang:

"If you're sad and homesick,
And don't know what to do,
Ask your buddy and you'll find
Your buddy's there for...Y-O-U!"

Coach stopped singing.

"Everybody freeze!" he shouted.

"Don't peek!" said Lady Lobelia. "Class I, take a step forward."

Wiglaf smelled that sweet scent again.

"Now, Class II, step forward," said Lady Lobelia.

Wiglaf stepped forward. The sweet scent grew stronger.

"Open your eyes," said Lady Lobelia. "And say hello to your buddy!"

Wiglaf opened his eyes. Yes!

Directly across from him, Grock opened his small yellow eyes.

The sweet scent was really strong now.

Wiglaf smiled. It had to be hard being the only troll at DSA. It had to be hard being so much bigger than everyone else. He was ready to start helping the troll right away.

"Hello, Grock," he said, looking up.

"Put 'er there, buddy!" said Grock. He held out a hairy hand.

Wiglaf reached out and shook the troll's hand.

"Yikes!" he cried as something in the troll's hand buzzed, giving his hand a shock. He quickly drew his hand away.

"Guh-huh! Guh-huh!" the troll laughed. He opened his hand to reveal an angry bumblebee. "Gotcha with me bee buzzer, buddy!"

Chapter 4

ver here, buddy!" Grock called to Wiglaf from the front of the breakfast line the following morning. "I saved ye a place, didn't I?"

"Thanks," said Wiglaf, slipping into line. He saw that the troll had stuffed his tunic pockets with packets of Frypot's red pepper sauce. Again, Wiglaf noticed the sweet, flowery smell.

Wiglaf felt a tap on the shoulder. He turned and saw Torblad behind him with his buddy, Aggie.

"No cutting," said Torblad.

"Let it go this time, Torblad," said Wiglaf.

But Torblad shook his head. "Go to the end of the line."

Wiglaf wondered, was Torblad really a stickler

for the rules? Or was he bothered by the troll's strong scent? What did Grock smell like, exactly? Clover, maybe? Or parsley?

"Hey, guy," Grock said to Torblad. "Ye've got a bug in yer ear."

"A bug?" shrieked Torblad. He began poking his fingers into his ears. "Which ear?"

Grock moved his lips as if he were speaking, but made no sound.

"What? What?" cried Torblad. "I can't hear you!"

And Grock shouted, "THAT'S 'CAUSE YE HAVE A BUG IN YER EAR!"

Torblad began jumping up and down and pounding on the side of his head.

Grock reached out to Torblad's left ear. He drew his hand away and opened it to reveal a HUGE cockroach.

"Aaaaiiii!" screamed Torblad, and he ran from the dining hall.

"In you go, Crawler," the troll said as he slid

the roach into the pocket of his tunic. He grinned at Wiglaf. "He's me pet."

"If you want to make friends, you have to stop tricking everybody, Grock," said Wiglaf.

"He deserved it, didn't he?" asked the troll.

"That was great, Grock," said Aggie. She slapped the troll on the back. "Can I sit with you at breakfast?"

"Yah," said Grock. "Why not?"

Wiglaf, Grock, and Aggie all helped themselves to Frypot's scrambled eel and moat-weed "bacon."

At the table, Erica was chatting with Dudwin, her Class I buddy Wiglaf felt very glad that Erica would be looking out for his little brother. Janice was trying to talk to her buddy, Maggot. And there was Angus, sitting next to Bilge, looking miserable.

"The food here is pretty bad!" Aggie said as they took their seats.

"Yah," said Grock. He shoveled his food into his mouth in one large clump. Then he chewed, with his mouth wide open, drooling. "How do ye stand it, buddy?"

"You get used to it," said Wiglaf, looking away so as not to see the chunks of half-chewed food spilling out of Grock's mouth. "So," he managed. "Do either of you have any questions about DSA?"

"Yah," said Grock. "Yer brother says ye slew two dragons. How did ye do it, buddy? Did ye whack 'em and stab 'em and slice off their bloody heads?"

"No!" said Wiglaf quickly. "I cannot stand the sight of blood."

"Ye can't?" said Grock.

Wiglaf shook his head. "I discovered the dragons' secret weaknesses," he said. "That's how I slew them."

"Whoops!" Grock said, dropping his spoon. He ducked under the table to get it.

"I have a question," said Aggie. "Who teaches music class?"

"We don't have music class," said Wiglaf.

"WHAT?" cried Aggie. "Mordred told my mother there was. I have to exercise my voice every single day."

"Found it!" Grock cried cheerily, popping up from beneath the table with his spoon. "I have another question, buddy. Can me mum send me a goodie box?"

"Sure," said Wiglaf. "My friend Angus gets goodie boxes from his mother all the time."

"Ah, good," said Grock. "'Cause me mum want to send me all the eyeballs."

"Is that a kind of candy?" asked Aggie.

"'Tis for me," said Grock, licking his lips with his pointy red tongue. "Eyeballs from all the humans she eats."

"Eww!" said Aggie. "You mean real eyeballs?"

"Yah," said Grock. "The fresh ones be nice and crunchy."

Wiglaf put down his spoon. He had lost his appetite. But Grock licked his plate clean.

"Can ye get seconds here?" Grock asked.

"I don't know," said Wiglaf. "No one's ever wanted seconds before."

Grock handed Wiglaf his plate. "Get me more, buddy. Pretty please with sugar on top?"

"All right." Wiglaf held the edges of Grock's slimy plate. He stood up and took a step toward the kitchen. *WHAP!* He fell flat on his face.

"Yow!" cried Wiglaf. The plate skidded across the floor.

"Guh-huh! Guh-huh! Guh-huh!" the troll laughed. "Have a nice trip, buddy?"

The dining hall erupted in laughter.

Erica ran over. "Wiggie!" she cried. "Are you okay?"

"I—I think so," said Wiglaf.

Dudwin was there, too. He and Erica helped Wiglaf sit up.

Wiglaf rubbed the bump that was rising on his forehead.

"Your boots!" cried Dudwin.

Wiglaf looked down. His boot laces had been tied together. No wonder he had tripped!

Erica untied the knot. "Wiggie!" she cried. "How did your boots get like this?"

"Ask my Class I buddy," said Wiglaf.

"Guh-huh! Guh-huh! Guh-huh!" Grock laughed. "Gotcha, buddy!"

"It's not funny, Grock," said Erica angrily. "Wiglaf could have really hurt himself."

"'Tis funny to me," said Grock. "Did ye see him go down? Thud!"

"Look, Grock, no more jokes," said Wiglaf.

"Aw right," said the troll. "But ye should have seen the look on yer face! Guh-huh, guh-huh!"

Wiglaf suffered through the rest of lunch.

Afterward, Grock said, "So, what's next?"

"Stalking class," Wiglaf said. He was still mad at Grock for making him trip.

"I don't know where my buddy went," said Aggie. "Can I come to class with you?"

"Sure," said Wiglaf. And he led the way through

the winding hallways of Dragon Slayers' Academy to the East Tower. He started up the spiraling stone staircase.

"Last one up is a rotten egg!" cried Grock. He pushed ahead of Wiglaf, taking the steps three at a time.

Aggie raced up after the troll. Wiglaf followed as fast as he could. When he was almost at the top of the steps, he heard horrible groaning sounds.

"What's wrong?" Wiglaf called, running faster. He leaped up the last step, and gasped.

Grock lay face up on the floor. The troll had a terrible head wound. Bright red blood dripped from his nose and his ears.

"Gahhhhh," Grock groaned.

"Wha—what happened?" cried Wiglaf. "Speak to me, Grock."

"He fell," said Aggie.

"Gahhhhh," Grock groaned again.

All the blood made Wiglaf's stomach churn. Still, he knelt down by the troll. He quickly untied his lucky rag from the hilt of his sword and tried to bind Grock's wound.

Grock's small yellow eyes popped open.

"Guh-huh! Guh-huh!" the troll laughed. "Gotcha, buddy!"

"What!" cried Wiglaf, drawing back.

The troll leaped to his feet.

"Red pepper sauce!" cried the troll. "I saved me packets. Guh-huh! Guh-huh!"

Aggie was laughing as hard as the troll.

"That's not funny, Grock!" said Wiglaf. "I thought you were hurt!"

"Yah," said Grock. "And, buddy? Troll blood isn't red. Me blood is black. And boiling hot. It'll make ye really sick to yer tum. Guh-huh, guh-huh!"

Wiglaf rose and stomped off to Dragon Stalking class. As far as he was concerned, having Grock for his buddy was no laughing matter.

Chapter 5

All the lads and lasses in Dragon Stalking class were in a line, holding on to a thick rope that hung out the window.

"One, two, three, heave ho!" Erica cried, and everyone pulled.

"What're they doing with the rope, buddy?" asked Grock.

Wiglaf didn't answer.

"Aw, come on, buddy," said Grock. "Ye aren't still mad, are ye?"

Wiglaf sighed. He was still mad. But he needed to get over it. "They're hoisting up Sir Mort," he told the troll. "He is very old, and cannot make it up the stairs in his suit of armor."

Grock raced over to the rope line. "Gimme

that!" he shouted, yanking the rope away from the other students.

"No!" said Angus. "It takes lots of us to pull Sir Mort up."

"Nah," said Grock. "I can do it meself."

"Let Grock do it," said Bilge. "He's strong!"

"Yeah!" said Maggot.

"Make way for Grock!" shouted Dudwin.

Grock began to tug on the rope. Everyone else let go. Hand over hand, the troll pulled, and soon Sir Mort's helmet appeared at the window.

For once, Sir Mort's visor was up. When he saw Grock's green face at the window, he cried, "Rattle my bones! Who are *you*?"

"Grock's me name," the troll said. He stopped pulling. "What'll ye give me to pull ye inside?"

"Grock!" cried Wiglaf. "Pull him in—now!"

Grock ignored his plea.

"What'll ye give me, teacher?" Grock said.

"Here's what I'll give you," said old Sir Mort as he dangled from the rope. "A swift kick in the backside if you don't hoist me in—now!"

Wiglaf grinned. The aged knight was fearless! But what if Grock dropped him?

"To the rope!" cried Wiglaf.

He and Janice and Erica and Dudwin and the others rushed the troll and yanked away the rope.

"Awwww, I was only fooling, wasn't I?" said Grock.

Wiglaf and the others gave one last pull and hoisted Sir Mort himself through the window. Then they helped the old knight to his feet and he clanked up to the front of the classroom.

"Bubbles von Troubles has been seen in the Swamp River near Toenail," Sir Mort announced.

"Oh, woe is Toenail!" cried Torblad.

"The dragon is said to be heading south. Or... is it north?" The old knight scratched his helmet. "The thing is, he's on his way to DSA."

"Why do you think Bubbles is coming here, sir?" Erica asked.

"He's after me, of course," said Sir Mort.

"Guh-huh! Guh-huh! Guh-huh!" Grock laughed. "Why would a dragon come after a geezer like ye?"

Sir Mort drew himself up tall. "In my glory days, I slew Bubbles's mate, Duckie McScales," he said. "Slew isn't quite the word. But I put her out of commission. Duckie was an enormous water dragon. She came at me with her duckbill open wide—a bill lined with razor-sharp fangs. Duckie chomped down and nearly bit off my right arm. Or...was it my left?"

"But, sir," said Erica.

"I drew my sword," said Sir Mort, keeping on with his story. "And I jabbed Duckie in the abdo-shrinka-dinka-puss. Right here." He pointed to a dragon's belly on a wall chart and made a sword-thrusting motion with his left arm.

"But, sir!" called Erica.

Sir Mort kept talking. "That dragon gave a terrible quack, and then she started shrinking.

When a fire-breathing dragon dies, it turns to dragon dust. But when a water-spewing dragon dies, it shrinks. And Duckie shrank down, down, down until she was no bigger than a bath toy." He chuckled. "I keep her in a drawer now. On a sunny day, I like to take her outside and give her a little float on the moat."

"SIR!" shouted Erica. "*In Famous Knights and Their Deeds*, it says that Duckie McScales was slain by Sir Trom, the brave and bold."

Wiglaf remembered reading that on the message tree.

Sir Mort clattered over to the chalkboard and wrote: T-R-O-M.

"Spell it backward, lads and lasses," said the old knight.

As the students spelled, the old knight wrote: M-O-R-T.

"Trom is Mort, spelled backward?" said Wiglaf.

"Bingo!" said Sir Mort. "Once, I was Sir Trom.

I slew more dragons before breakfast than most knights slay in a year."

All the students gasped. Their ancient teacher had once been the boldest knight alive!

The old knight frowned. "Then Bubbles came after me to get revenge. No matter where I went, he found me. I went questing in the mountains. Bubbles quested after me. I sailed off to a desert island. Bubbles swam after me. That's why I changed my name."

"Did it stop Bubbles, sir?" asked Angus.

"Yes, indeed!" Sir Mort smiled. "Sir Trom disappeared from the face of the earth. And Bubbles couldn't find him."

"Then why is he coming after you now, sir?" asked Wiglaf.

The smile faded from Sir Mort's ancient lips. "Last week, there was an article in *The Medieval Times* on the world's oldest living knights," he told the class. "There were drawings of Sir Roger and Sir Poodleduff and me on the front page. Bubbles must have seen the paper and recognized me. For from the very day my picture appeared, I began hearing rumors that Bubbles was getting closer and closer to Dragon Slayers' Academy."

Wiglaf frowned. He remembered something else he had read on the message tree flyer. Bubbles was very dangerous. Poor Sir Mort!

"Have no fear, Sir Mort!" cried Erica. "We shall slay this dragon for you!"

"What's his secret weakness?" called Dudwin.

"Something to do with his sniffer," answered Sir Mort. "He is said to have a very sensitive nose. More than that I know not."

Wiglaf thought back to the flyer about Bubbles on the message tree. After "Secret weakness" all it said was "Ah-ah-ah-ah..." What did that have to do with his nose?

Just then Grock bolted out of his seat and ran to the window. "Teacher!" he called. "Is Bubbles a big blue dragon?"

"Why, yes, he is," said Sir Mort.

"Teacher!" called Grock. "Do Bubbles have a big red horn on his forehead?"

"He does!" cried Sir Mort. "Oh, Bubbles toots a mean boogie-woogie on that horn while he gobbles up his victims."

"Teacher!" called Grock. "Do Bubbles like to do fancy swims?"

"Yes! Bubbles is a great show-off," said Sir Mort.

Wiglaf ran to the window. But Grock stepped in front of it, blocking his way.

"Is Bubbles out there, Grock?" said Wiglaf. "Or is this another trick?"

"See for yerself, buddy," said Grock, stepping aside.

Wiglaf ran to the window and stuck his head out. He looked down at the castle moat.

"I don't see any dragon," said Wiglaf.

"Look harder, buddy!" said Grock.

Wiglaf leaned farther out the window. All of a sudden he felt a push—and he felt himself falling headfirst out the window.

"Aiiiiii!" Wiglaf cried. "Help!"

A pair of strong hands gripped his ankles, holding him upside down.

"Do ye see the dragon yet, buddy?" asked Grock.

"No!" cried Wiglaf. He was so scared, he couldn't see anything.

Wiglaf heard Dudwin shouting, "Pull my brother up, Grock!"

"Like this?" asked Grock, shaking him up and down.

"Stooooop!" cried Wiglaf. He squeezed his eyes shut. He didn't want to die. Not like this!

"I'll stop when ye say ye see the dragon!" said Grock.

"N-n-no!" Wiglaf cried.

Now Wiglaf heard Sir Mort's voice: "Hoist 'im in, lad."

"Now, Grock," Erica growled. "Or you shall feel more than the point of my sword!"

"Owie!" yelped Grock. "Hurts!"

Suddenly Wiglaf felt himself being yanked up,

up, up. He hit the cold stone floor.

"Wiggie?" cried Dudwin. "Are you all right?"

"Uuggh," Wiglaf groaned.

Grock glared at Erica.

"Ye wounded me!" he cried. "Look." Grock rolled up his sleeve and showed everyone the back of his arm. There was a tiny bump on it no bigger than a bug bite. It wasn't even bleeding.

"You'll live, Grock," said Erica.

"Yah," said Grock. "But it hurts!" He looked as if he were about to cry.

The end-of-class bell rang.

"Till tomorrow, lads and lasses," Sir Mort called as his students trailed out of the classroom. "I'll show you how I plan to slay Bubbles with the old sword-and-dagger switcheroo. Excellent way to confuse a dragon. Works every time."

Angus steadied Wiglaf and helped him out of class. Grock stuck by Wiglaf's other side.

"I was only trying to help ye see the dragon, buddy," he said.

"I don't believe that," Wiglaf managed.

"Yah, really, I was," said the troll. "Don't ye trust me, buddy?"

Wiglaf had felt sorry for Grock, the lone troll at DSA. He had tried to be his friend, to be a good buddy. But did he trust the troll?

"No, I don't trust you, Grock," Wiglaf said.

"I don't trust you, either," said Angus.

Grock grinned. "Good move," he said, and he ran off, laughing.

Wiglaf had fallen into Stinking Green Creek and nearly drowned. He had been held in a dragon's paw and nearly squeezed to death. But as he walked down the East Tower stairs, he thought that being around Grock was even worse. The troll had made Wiglaf look like a great big fool.

Chapter 6

"Where to now, buddy?" Grock asked, catching up with Wiglaf on the stairs.

"I'm going to the library. You don't have to come," Wiglaf said hopefully.

"Yah, I do," said Grock. "We buddies sticks together."

"You'd better behave, Grock," said Wiglaf. "Brother Dave, the DSA librarian, is really nice."

Grock grinned. "I love good books."

Wiglaf led Grock to DSA's South Tower. What sort of books did Grock love? Probably *Mean Tricks* and *More Mean Tricks*. By the time they had climbed up the 427 steps, Wiglaf was winded. But Grock ran up the steps as if they were nothing.

"Brother Dave?" called Wiglaf.

A little monk with round spectacles rushed out from behind a bookshelf.

"Wiglaf!" cried Brother Dave. "How glad I art to see thee! Thou hast grown taller over the summer!"

"Really?" asked Wiglaf happily.

Brother Dave nodded. "And who hast thou brought with thee?"

"My Class I buddy. His name is Grock," said Wiglaf.

"I welcome thee to DSA, Grock," said Brother Dave. "I hopest thou shalt be very happy here."

Suddenly the troll's eyes grew wide. He yelped and scurried behind a bookcase.

"What ails thee, lad?" called Brother Dave.

"Dragon!" shouted Grock. "Green dragon!"

"Is it Worm?" Wiglaf ran to the window slit, hoping to see the young dragon he and Angus had raised from piplinghood. But the sky was empty. "What dragon, Grock?" said Wiglaf. "You're lying again, aren't you?"

"On floor," Grock called from behind the bookcase.

"That's only a pillow, Grock," Wiglaf said. "Take a look."

Grock peeked out from behind the bookcase. He looked warily at the large green dragon-shaped pillow that Brother Dave had made. Its long, forked pink tongue was made of felt. It had white felt claws and fangs, too.

Grock came out from his hiding place. But he was trembling a little.

Wiglaf caught a whiff of a strong, spicy odor. It tickled his nose and he sneezed.

"Bless thee, lad," said Brother Dave.

"You don't need to be afraid," Wiglaf said.

"Me? Afraid? Guh-huh, guh-huh!" laughed Grock. "I knew it was a faker dragon. I was fooling."

But Wiglaf wondered: Underneath his tough troll hide, was Grock really a scaredy-troll?

"Browseth around, Grock," Brother Dave said,

"Wiglaf and I must catcheth up for a moment."

As the troll wandered off, Brother Dave opened his desk drawer and took out a book.

"This once belongeth to my great-great grandfather," said Brother Dave. "He passeth it down to my great-grandfather, who passeth it down to my grandfather, who passeth it down to my father, who passeth it down to me. I would very much like to giveth it to thee, Wiglaf."

Wiglaf read the title: *A Knight and His Dragon.*

"'Tis a story about a knight who findeth a dragon egg, lad," said Brother Dave. "The knight and his dragon haveth many a fine adventure."

"Oh, thank you, Brother Dave!" said Wiglaf.

"Thou art welcome, lad," said Brother Dave, handing over the book. "Worm cameth to see me last week," he added.

"How is he?" asked Wiglaf, eager for any news of his beloved dragon.

"Oh, how he hast grown!" said Brother Dave. "Thou wouldst not know—" He stopped and listened. "Dost thou hearest an odd crunching sound?"

Wiglaf listened. "I hear something," he said. "Grock!" he cried and turned to Brother Dave. "I fear that troll is up to no good. Grock!" he called. "Grock!"

Grock did not answer.

Now Brother Dave put a finger to his lips.

The two of them listened. There was the crunching again.

They tiptoed toward the back of the library. There, between two bookshelves, was the troll.

Brother Dave gasped. "Oh, Grock! What hast thou done?"

"Grock!" cried Wiglaf. "No!"

Grock smiled up at them from where he sat on the floor, surrounded by a huge pile of torn-up books.

"Yah, Brother!" said Grock. "Ye have really good books up here!" He took a bite out of the book he was holding and chewed loudly.

"Please stoppeth!" cried Brother Dave. "Taketh not another bite!"

"One more." Grock took another bite. "Yummers!"

"Books are for reading!" Wiglaf cried.

"Fer ye, maybe," said Grock. "But I eats 'em." Grock held his tummy and let out a belch.

"Goest thou from this library, Grock," Brother Dave said sternly.

Wiglaf had never seen the little monk so upset.

"Yah, all right," said the troll. "But can I check out some books?"

"Thou mayest not," said Brother Dave.

Grock's tummy rumbled loudly.

"I ate me books too fast!" he wailed. He burped again. "I need to lie down. Come on, buddy. Ye got to put me to bed."

"Put yourself to bed, Grock," said Wiglaf.

"No!" cried Grock. "Buddies sticks together!" His tummy rumbled again. It sounded like thunder.

Wiglaf shook his head.

Grock moaned. Then he turned and ran down the 427 steps clutching his tummy.

Wiglaf helped Brother Dave clean up the pile of half-eaten books.

"Mine fellow monks of the Little Brothers of the Peanut Brittle loveth to maketh copies," said Brother Dave. "In ten or twelve years, we shalt havest these books on our shelves once more."

"I'm sorry about this," said Wiglaf.

"It art not thy fault, lad," said Brother Dave. "Thou didst not knowest." The little monk looked thoughtful. "If he hast not eaten it, I haveth a book that may helpeth thee with thou buddy."

Brother Dave scurried off. When he returned, he held a copy of a small, leather-bound book: *All About Trolls.*

Brother Dave opened it. "Readeth this, Wiglaf," he said, and he handed him the book.

TOP TEN TROLL TIPS

10. A troll is as strong as six humans, three ogres, or half a giant.

9. A troll has big feet with any number of toes, and never wears shoes.

8. A happy troll smells strongly of peppermint.

Wiglaf looked up from the book. "That's what Grock smells like!" he exclaimed. "Peppermint!"

"Ah," said Brother Dave. "I smelleth it, too. It art a pleasing scent."

Wiglaf nodded, thinking that when Grock had been frightened of the dragon pillow, his scent had changed. It was not minty at all, but strong and spicy.

Wiglaf read on:

7. A troll does not like sunlight, but prefers to lurk about at night, under a bridge or in a cave.

6. A troll loves nothing more than making mischief.

5. A troll is always hungry and will eat almost

anything, including sticks, stones, books, and worms.

4. A troll's thick, black blood will burn a human on contact.

3. A troll will do anything to get out of doing work.

2. A troll enjoys telling whoppers and playing nasty pranks.

1. Never trust a troll.

"If only I had read this book before I brought Grock up here!" said Wiglaf.

Brother Dave smiled kindly and said, "Thou never knowest what good mayest yet cometh from thine difficult Class I buddy."

Chapter 7

"Up and at 'em, lads!" called Frypot, banging two cooking pots together. "'Tis another beautiful day at Dragon Slayers' Academy."

Wiglaf rolled out of his cot. He was sleepy this morning. He had borrowed Erica's mini-torch and stayed up late, reading *A Knight and His Dragon*. It was the best book he had ever read. He couldn't wait to find out whether the knight and his dragon would defeat the evil sorcerer and his griffin.

Wiglaf tucked the book into his belt. He hoped to find a few minutes during the day to read another chapter. As he pulled on his tunic, he smelled peppermint. So when his head poked out of the neck hole, he was not surprised to see the troll. He noticed that Grock's own tunic was spotted with stains from every meal he'd gobbled down at DSA.

"Breakfast time, buddy," said Grock. He had a pack slung over his shoulder this morning.

"Ready," Wiglaf said.

The two set off for the dining hall. On the way, Aggie, Dudwin, Bilge, and Maggot joined them. "Why aren't you with your Class II buddies?" Wiglaf asked them.

"They're boring," said Bilge.

"Yeah," said Maggot.

"We'd rather be with you and Grock, Wiggie," said Dudwin.

"Mostly Grock," said Aggie. "He is so cool!"

"Yah," said Grock.

"What'll it be, lads and lass?" Frypot asked when they stepped up in the breakfast line. "Eel-bean burritos? Or eel waffles with moat syrup?"

"Both!" cried Grock, holding out his plate.

"Both!" said the Class I copycats, holding out their plates.

Wiglaf looked at the pile of slimy burritos. And at the dark brown waffles swimming in what had to be mud.

"Waffle," he said, feeling sick as he said it.

Grock led the way to a table. Aggie and Dudwin sprang into the seats next to the troll.

"No fair," said Bilge. "You guys sat next to Grock at supper."

The troll picked up the burrito and shoved the whole thing into his mouth. Juice leaked out and ran down his chin as he chewed.

Dudwin and the other Class I copycats shoved their whole burritos into their mouths. Maggot nearly choked on his and had to burp it up. Disgusting!

Wiglaf sighed. It was bad enough having one buddy. Now he suddenly had five! This was going to be a long week.

"So, buddy," Grock said two days later at lunch, his mouth stuffed with Frypot's eel potpie, "what next?"

"Yeah," said Maggot. "What's next?"

"Dragon Science class," said Wiglaf. "With Professor Pluck."

"Science, pooey!" said Grock. "I wants to slay a dragon. I wants to slay Bubbles!"

"Me too!" said Bilge. "I want to slay lots of dragons!"

"Yeah," said Maggot. "Me too."

"Uh, me three," said Dudwin.

"I'm in, too," said Aggie. "I guess."

"Right now, we have to go to class," said Wiglaf. "And we have to get there early to get seats in the back. Professor Pluck is a spitter. If you sit up front, you get spat upon."

"Eww!" said Aggie.

But Grock grinned. "I'd like to see that, wouldn't I?"

Grock pulled his roach out of his pocket and put him on the table. "Go on, Crawler," he said.

The roach dashed over to Wiglaf's plate and

ran across his eel potpie.

"Ugh!" said Wiglaf, pushing his plate away.

"Oh, ye don't want that?" said Grock, pocketing his roach. He grabbed the plate and gobbled up the potpie. He licked the plate. Then he ate the plate.

His Class I posse cracked up.

When lunch finally ended, Wiglaf led the way to the North Tower.

"**P**lease come in, **pup**ils!" the professor said, spewing spit each time he said the letter *P*. "**P**ut down your **p**acks, **p**ick u**p** a **p**iece of **p**archment, and **p**ick a **p**lace to **p**erch."

Wiglaf picked up a parchment. On it were two drawings of a water dragon. A drawing titled "Before Drinking" showed the dragon with a small stomach. A drawing titled "After Drinking" showed a dragon with its stomach expanded into an enormous round ball.

Wiglaf looked up from the parchment.

"Let's take those two seats in the last row,

Grock," he said.

When the troll did not answer, Wiglaf turned. The troll had been right beside him a second ago. Now where was he?

"**P**laces **p**lease, **pup**ils!" spewed Professor Pluck. "I am a **p**unctual **p**rofessor. I **p**refer to start **p**rom**p**tly."

Wiglaf sniffed. He could smell the pepperminty troll. But he didn't see him anywhere.

"**P**laces!" said Professor Pluck.

Wiglaf hurried to the back of the room. He was about to sit down when an unseen force picked him up.

"Yaaaah!" cried Wiglaf as the force rushed him to the front of the room and plunked him down in a front-row seat.

"A **p**upil **up** front," sputtered Professor Pluck, beaming at Wiglaf. "**P**erfect! Now, **p**ay attention, **pup**ils! Most dragons **s**pew fire. Today I will **s**peak about a **p**eculiar ty**p**e that **s**pews water."

Professor Pluck was spewing water himself.

Sprays of spit hit Wiglaf's face. Yuck! He tried to get up, but something held him down.

"Pay special attention to the top of your parchment," said Professor Pluck. "This shows a picture of a small water dragon lapping up pounds and pounds of water. The pouch inside its paunch expands with water until it is perfectly huge. Then it sprays the water out at stupendous force."

Water droplets ran down Wiglaf's cheeks and neck. His carrot-colored hair was soaking wet and stuck to his head. He was miserable.

"A water dragon," said Professor Pluck, "can drain a moat faster than you can say 'Peter Piper picked a peck of pickles peppers.' "

As Professor Pluck sputtered on about water dragons, Wiglaf heard a familiar sound: "Guh-huh! Guh-huh! Guh-huh!"

"Grock!" he whispered. "Where are you?"

"Right by ye, buddy," Grock growled. "Ye looks funny all wet."

Suddenly a burst of sparks erupted next

to Wiglaf.

"Yaaaaaah!" came the troll's voice as more sparks flew. "Ouchie!"

"**Prince Peter's p**laid **p**ants!" exclaimed Professor Pluck.

"'Tis a bad omen!" cried Torblad. "We are doomed!"

Now Wiglaf understood what was happening. Somehow Grock had found Dudwin's magic cap of invisibility!

Sparks shot in all directions.

"Yahhhh!" yelled Grock. "Owww! Hurts me!"

"Say 'Zappity Zip,' Grock!" called Dudwin.

"Zap-owie!" cried the troll.

One big green many-toed foot appeared. Then it vanished. The troll's other foot appeared, and disappeared. The troll's belly began to flash on and off.

The students in Dragon Science were laughing their heads off.

A huge explosion of sparks lit the science lab.

"Owwwwwie!" squealed Grock.

Wiglaf couldn't see Grock, but he could smell that strong, spicy scared-troll smell again. It made him sneeze.

Grock's arm flashed into being, and stayed visible. And when the troll's big head appeared, Wiglaf knew what to do. He grabbed the cap and pulled it off Grock's head.

"That was great, Grock!" called Bilge.

"Yeah!" called Maggot.

"What a show!" called Aggie.

Dudwin jumped to his feet and clapped.

Grock grinned and took a bow. Then he turned to Wiglaf.

"Give me cap back, buddy," he said. "It's mine."

"No, it isn't," said Wiglaf as the cap shot its last few sparks.

"I don't want it," said Dudwin. "Grock can have it."

"Pupils, please!" sputtered Professor Pluck.

"Stop! Let me speak."

But before Professor Pluck could sputter another word, the door to his classroom flew open and a large duck waddled in.

"'Tis Duckie McScales come for revenge!" screamed Torblad.

"Nah," said the duck. "'Tis only me, Yorick."

Mordred's scout, Yorick, was the master of disguise. He traveled around and heard things and saw things. He brought what he learned back to DSA.

Now Yorick ripped off his duckbill and his feathered headdress.

"Gets bloody hot under these feathers," he said. "I have news!"

"Pray, tell!" said Professor Pluck.

"I have waddled far and near," said Yorick. "I have paddled upstream and down. I have swum in lakes, ponds, and puddles."

Wiglaf knew if Mordred were there, he would have shouted, "Get to the point, man!"

But Mordred wasn't there, so Yorick rambled on for quite a while before he said, "And every tree by every stream and creek and lake and river, is marked with the letter *B*."

"Bubbles!" cried Dudwin. "That's his sign!"

"Aye," said Yorick. "And Bubbles is swimming this way. Heading straight for Dragon Slayers' Academy."

Grock ran to the slit in the castle wall and looked down.

"Bubbles is in the moat!" he shouted. "He's here!"

"Do you see Bubbles, Grock?" Wiglaf called. "Or is this another joke?"

"Bubbles in the moat!" cried the troll. "Honest!"

Wiglaf didn't trust Grock one bit. But now he heard wild splashing and yelling from below. Maybe this time, the troll was telling the truth.

Chapter 8

"Dragon in the moat!" Mordred shouted from the castle yard below. "To arms, lads and lasses! To arms!"

"To the moat!" cried Erica. "We shall vanquish this dragon!"

All the lads and lasses raced from Professor Pluck's classroom.

"Please put the parchments in a pile as you depart!" Professor Pluck sputtered after them.

"I'll stick with ye, buddy," said Grock as they ran down the spiraling stairs, through the castle hallways, and out into the castle yard.

Wiglaf caught a whiff of the troll's strong, spicy odor.

"Slay the dragon and get his gold!" Mordred

instructed them as they ran across the castle yard. "I'll be watching from my office."

With that, the headmaster ran up the castle steps and out of sight.

The lads and lasses raced over the drawbridge. Coach Plungett stood at the foot of it.

"Remember the Throat Thrust!" he coached.

"I don't see Bubbles," said Angus as they took their places beside the moat.

"Me either," said Dudwin.

"Maybe he's hiding in the part of the moat hidden behind the castle," said Wiglaf.

"Shall we rush him?" asked Janice.

"Yeah!" said Maggot and Bilge.

"No!" said Erica. "Let Bubbles swim out and see the band of mighty warriors who await him."

"Good idea," said Wiglaf. "Where are they?"

"*We* are the mighty warriors, Wiggie," said Erica.

Grock stood next to Wiglaf. For a change, he was silent.

Wiglaf turned to him. The troll looked nervous. And the air was filled with his spicy scent.

"What's wrong, Grock?" asked Wiglaf.

"Nothing, buddy," said Grock.

Now Sir Mort came tottering over the drawbridge. He held a sword in one hand and a dagger in the other, ready to confuse Bubbles with the switcheroo. The old knight's visor was down. Wiglaf wondered whether he could see, for he was tottering badly.

"Back off, lads and lasses!" shouted Sir Mort. "Make way for a real knight to fight his old foe!"

Then Sir Mort took a wrong step, and toppled into the moat. Armored as he was, he sank fast.

"We'll save you!" cried Wiglaf. He leaped into the moat. So did Erica, Angus, Janice, and Dudwin. Together, they managed to pull Sir Mort up.

Coach Plungett took the old knight and laid him down on the grass.

"Get his armor off," said Coach.

Erica wrested off his helmet. Wiglaf unbuckled

his breastplate. Angus took off his armored sleeves. Erica held Sir Mort's armored boots while Janice pulled off his leg armor. Sir Mort looked very small lying there in his red long underwear. At last he opened his eyes and said, "Ah, the old switcheroo. Works every time."

"I'll take him inside to dry off," Coach said. He slung Sir Mort over his shoulder and hurried to the castle.

"I think I see Bubbles!" someone yelled.

"Yes! Yes! There he is!" others shouted.

Wiglaf caught sight of Grock running away from the moat. The troll ducked behind a large rock to hide.

Wiglaf ran after him. "What's wrong, Grock?" he asked. "Don't you want to fight the dragon with us?"

"Busy right now, buddy," called Grock from behind the rock.

Once more the scared-troll spicy odor made Wiglaf sneeze. He turned back to the moat just in time to see a shiny blue dragon swim out from behind the castle.

Bubbles.

Wiglaf was surprised that he was so small—not much bigger than Daisy! He had a friendly smile on his face. The red horn on top of his head was tooting a peppy tune.

Wiglaf ran back and joined the others standing beside the moat.

"I told you Bubbles wasn't scary, Wiggie," said Dudwin. "Look at him!"

"He doesn't *look* scary," Wiglaf admitted. "But looks aren't everything, Dud."

"Hallo, lads and lasses!" Bubbles called out. "Thank you all for coming out to greet me!"

"We are not here to greet you, Bubbles!" shouted Erica.

"We are here to slay you!" cried Janice.

"Yeah!" cried Bilge and Maggot.

"Don't be silly," said Bubbles. "I mean you no harm. I only want to settle an old score with one of your teachers, that's all."

Bubbles swam as he spoke. As he came closer, Wiglaf saw that the dragon wore a gold chain around his neck. Hanging from the chain was a golden letter *B*. It glittered against the dragon's blue scales.

"Want to see something great?" asked Bubbles, blinking his bright blue eyes. "Watch this."

Bubbles flipped over onto his back. He stuck one webbed foot up into the air and pointed his claws. Then his leg sank slowly until the claws disappeared. The moat water bubbled like crazy.

Suddenly, Bubbles burst up out of the water, spinning like a top. He stopped spinning, and cried, "Tah-dah!"

"That was super!" called Bilge.

"Yeah!" called Maggot.

"Do it again!" called Dudwin, clapping.

"Class I!" yelled Erica. "Do not be fooled! Bubbles is dangerous!"

"Oh, come on," said Aggie. "Look at him.

He's cute!"

Bubbles smiled and blinked his big blue eyes. "Want to see more?"

"Yes!" cried the Class I lads and lasses.

"More!" cried Grock, running out from behind the rock. "More, dragon!" He ran to the edge of the moat.

Bubbles sniffed and wrinkled his nose, as if he smelled something he didn't like. Then he dove under the water and came up again some distance away from Grock.

"Here I go!" called Bubbles. "Watch this!"

The dragon swam in a circle, fluttering one wing over the water. He did a porpoise dive and disappeared. Then he came up again, feet first, laying himself calmly on top of the water. Next, he began twisting and turning and flipping like a seal.

Wiglaf had to admit that Bubbles had talent. He began to wonder—was Bubbles really dangerous?

When the dragon finished his water ballet, he swam to the edge of the moat closest to Erica.

"You seem to be in charge here, lass," he said.

"You got that right, Bubbles!" said Erica.

"Then will you be so kind as to ask Sir Trom to come out here for a moment?" he asked.

"Bubbles," said Erica. "You have two choices. You can go away and never come back. Or we can slay you. You decide."

Bubbles smiled. "No. YOU have two choices," he said. "You can go and get Sir Trom, or—"

Erica cut him off. "Never!" she cried.

"Have it your way, lass," said Bubbles.

The dragon dipped his mouth into the moat.

Wiglaf heard a loud sucking sound. The water in the moat began to get shallower and shallower. Eels started jumping all over the place.

As the level of the water in the moat went down, Bubbles's body grew bigger and bigger. His head looked small now on top of his great, bloated belly.

"Yahhhh!" cried Grock as the dragon expanded.

He ran back to his hiding place behind the rock.

Bubbles grew to an enormous size. When he had sucked nearly all the water out of the moat, Professor Pluck stuck his head out of the slit in the castle wall. He shouted, "**P**eter **P**iper **p**icked a **p**eck of **p**ickled **p**eppers!"

Bubbles raised his head. Now he was almost as huge as the DSA castle.

"GET SIR TROM!" Bubbles bellowed. "OR GET YOUR SURFBOARDS—YOU DECIDE!"

Chapter 9

"Hold it! Hold it!" Mordred came running down the drawbridge. "Don't go flooding my school, Bubbles. Let's talk!"

"WHO ARE YOU?" asked Bubbles.

"Mordred de Marvelous," said Mordred. "Headmaster of Dragon Sla—errr, this school. This fellow you call Sir Trom is one of my teachers."

"SEND SIR TROM OUT NOW!" Bubbles shouted. "OR MEET A WATERY DOOM!"

"Sir Mort—er, Sir Trom—has had an unfortunate accident," said Mordred. "Fell into the moat and knocked himself out."

"BRING HIM TO ME," said Bubbles.

"I could do that," said Mordred. "If you promise not to send a tidal wave over my castle."

"YOU HAVE MY WORD," said the dragon.

"All right," said Mordred. "I'll have someone carry him outside."

"Sir! No!" cried Wiglaf. "You can't do that!"

"It wouldn't be a fair fight!" called Erica.

"It would be shabby!" called Janice.

"For shame, Uncle Mordred!" called Angus.

"Oh, be quiet, you little goodie-goodies," said Mordred. He chewed on his fingernails for a moment, thinking. "Listen, Bubbles," he said at last. "I'll get Sir Mort up. I'll walk him around. Get a little java into him. He should be fit as a fiddle by tomorrow morning, and he'll come out and fight you then. Do we have a deal?"

"NO," thundered Bubbles. "HE MUST COME TONIGHT. BY MIDNIGHT."

"Right-o!" said Mordred. "He'll be here. Now, would you mind refilling the moat? Hate to lose my eels. My students refuse to eat anything else."

"NO PROBLEM," said Bubbles.

Mordred ran back into the castle.

The dragon bent down toward the moat. He opened up his mouth and a gusher flowed forth. In a very short time, the moat was full again. And the eels were jumping—this time, for joy.

Bubbles was Daisy-size again. He floated happily on the moat.

"More tricks, Bubbles!" called Dudwin.

"Give us another show!" called Bilge.

"Yeah," called Maggot.

"We're your fans, Bubbles!" called Aggie.

Bubbles smiled. He stretched out on his back and began doing the flutter kick.

The Class II lads and lasses retreated to the far side of the drawbridge to make a plan.

"We must get rid of Bubbles before midnight," said Erica.

"Or Sir Mort is a goner," added Janice.

"What can we do?" asked Angus.

Wiglaf spotted Grock peering out from behind the rock.

"Hey, buddy!" the troll called, hurrying

toward him.

Wiglaf could smell the spicy scent of the troll before he reached them.

"What smells?" asked Erica.

"Grock," whispered Wiglaf. "He smells like that when he gets scared."

"Smells like pepper," said Angus, and he sneezed: *AH-CHOO!*

Pepper! thought Wiglaf as Grock drew closer. *That's exactly what Grock smells like.*

Suddenly the parchment on the message tree came to mind again.

"That could be it," Wiglaf murmured to himself.

"What could be it, Wiggie?" asked Erica.

"Tell you later," said Wiglaf as Grock came closer.

Maybe, just maybe, Wiglaf understood what it meant when it said Bubbles's secret weakness was *Ah-ah-ah-ah...*

"I'm going back for my biggest lance," said Janice.

"I'm going to get my deluxe edition Sir Lancelot sword," said Erica.

"I'm going to get some stash," said Angus.

The three jogged off toward the drawbridge.

"Look, buddy," the troll said to Wiglaf.

He opened his hand. On his palm sat a huge spider.

"Me new pet, Webster," said Grock. "Get it? Spider? Web-ster? Guh-huh! Guh-huh!"

"That's what you were doing behind the rock?" said Wiglaf. "Looking for bugs?"

"Yah," said Grock. "Found a friend for Crawler."

Wiglaf heard the sound of Dudwin and the other Class I lads and lasses cheering. Bubbles must have finished another show.

"Grock," said Wiglaf. "Are you afraid of dragons?"

"Don't make me laugh," said Grock. "Guh-huh! Guh-huh!"

"I am afraid of dragons," said Wiglaf.

"Yah?" said Grock.

Wiglaf nodded. "Everybody is," he said. "Except Erica, maybe," he added. "But not everybody runs away and hides behind a rock."

"I was looking for bugs, wasn't I?" said Grock.

"Sure," said Wiglaf. "What I'm saying is, you can be afraid and still fight a dragon. You can be a dragon slayer, Grock."

"I know that, don't I?" said Grock.

"You can be a dragon slayer tonight," said Wiglaf.

Grock did not look so sure anymore.

"You can slay Bubbles, Grock," said Wiglaf.

The words were hardly out of his mouth when a blast of peppery scent rose from the troll. Grock was afraid.

Wiglaf glanced up at the sky. A full moon was rising over the DSA castle. A few stars were popping out. Good. It would be easier to carry out the plan he had in mind if there was a little light.

"Stay here, Grock," said Wiglaf. "I'll be right back."

"I be over here," Grock said, and he scurried behind the rock again.

Wiglaf found the Class I lads and lasses watching Bubbles's latest water ballet performance.

"Hi, Wiggie," said Dudwin. "Watch Bubbles!"

"He's great!" shouted Bilge.

"Yeah!" shouted Maggot.

"You should see his clamshell dive," Aggie said. "Amazing."

Wiglaf watched the blue dragon curl up in a tuck position and do a series of somersaults just under the surface of the water.

As Bubbles spun, Wiglaf tapped Aggie on the shoulder. She turned toward him, and he put his finger to his lips.

Aggie nodded. She didn't say a word.

Wiglaf beckoned her over toward the woods. Quickly, he explained his plan to her.

Aggie smiled. "Help Grock? Sure. You can count on me!" she said.

"This plan may not work," said Wiglaf. "But we

must try it—to save Sir Mort."

Aggie nodded. "I shall make it work!" she said.

The two of them went back and watched the grand finale of Bubbles's show.

"Thank you, thank you," said Bubbles as they clapped for him.

Now Wiglaf cupped his hands to his mouth and called, "Bubbles?"

"Yes?" said the dragon.

"How about playing some music on your horn?" asked Wiglaf.

"Happy to," the dragon said. "Any requests?"

"'Blue Dragon,'" said Wiglaf.

Bubbles smiled. "Oh, I love that song! It's my favorite."

"Mine, too," Aggie said. "Mind if I sing along?"

Bubbles didn't answer. He was already playing the bluesy tune softly on his horn.

Aggie started singing the words:

"Once I was a fierce young dragon,
All the world was mine!
Once I was a lucky dragon,
Back then life was fine.

"Then I fell for you,
And when you said, 'We're through.'
What could I do?
But be blue, oh, so blue.
Now I'm a blue blue dragon..."

As quietly as he could, Wiglaf backed away, then he sneaked over to Grock's rock.

"Grock!" he whispered. "Come slay Bubbles."

"Nah, buddy," said Grock. "Not tonight."

"This is your one and only chance to become a dragon slayer," said Wiglaf.

Grock shook his head.

"Please! You have to!" said Wiglaf. "I—I'll give you something. Anything!"

Grock's little yellow eyes lit up. "What, buddy?"

Wiglaf had no pennies. He did not have much.

"Angus is bringing down some of his stash," said Wiglaf. "You like candy?"

"Nah," said Grock. "I like eyeballs, don't I?"

Wiglaf's mind was spinning. He had to think of something.

"My book!" he blurted out. "The one Brother Dave gave me."

"Is it a good book, buddy?" asked Grock.

"It's the best book ever," said Wiglaf. He couldn't stand to think of Grock taking a big bite out of *The Knight and His Dragon*. But he was desperate. He had to save Sir Mort.

"Mmmm, a good book," said Grock. He began to drool. "Okay, buddy, deal. What I have to do?"

"Sneak up on Bubbles while he's playing his horn," said Wiglaf. "Get really close."

The peppery smell began to rise from the troll.

"Will you do it, Grock?" asked Wiglaf.

"Yah, sure. I promise, buddy," said Grock. "Gimme yer book."

Wiglaf slipped *The Knight and His Dragon* from his belt. Now he'd never know how it ended. This book had belonged to Brother Dave's great-great-grandfather. How sad that it was going to end up as a troll snack.

Wiglaf held up the book. "You get this after you deal with Bubbles," he said.

"Nah," said the troll. "Now!"

"First the dragon," Wiglaf said firmly. "Then the book."

Chapter 10

Wiglaf stuck his book back under his belt. He grabbed Grock's hairy hand and led him quietly toward the moat.

Aggie and the dragon were still making music together. Wiglaf thought they sounded excellent.

"Once I was a happy dragon,
Flying through the clouds.
Once I was a snappy dragon,
Roaring oh so loud."

When they got close to the moat, Grock stopped. "Changed me mind, didn't I?" he said.

"You promised, Grock," whispered Wiglaf.

"I be a troll!" Grock whispered back. "I never keep me promises!"

"You're keeping this one, Grock," said Wiglaf. He didn't really need to ask—the peppery smell told him all he needed to know—but he did ask. "Are you afraid?"

Grock nodded. "Yah, buddy," he said.

Wiglaf pulled the troll toward Bubbles. "Be afraid..." said Wiglaf. "Be very afraid!"

Aggie was still singing when they reached the edge of the moat. Bubbles's eyes were closed. Wiglaf could tell he was really into playing.

"Once I was an angry dragon,
Lurking in my cave.
Once I was a fuming dragon,
Oh, how I did rave."

Wiglaf gave Grock the nod. The troll lumbered slowly toward the dragon.

All at once, Bubbles's nostrils started to twitch. But he kept on playing "Blue Dragon." And Aggie kept singing:

"Once I was a wicked dragon,
How villagers did flee!
Once I was a vicious dragon,
Not one worse than me.

"Then I fell for you,
And when you said, 'We're through.'
What could I do?
But be blue, oh, so blue."

Grock stepped into the shallow part of the moat. Bubbles's whole snout was quivering now. But still he played his horn.

Grock stepped closer...and closer.

A few of the Class I lads and lasses sneezed.

Aggie belted out the "Blue Dragon" chorus, while Bubbles played a complicated riff on his horn:

"Now I'm a blue, blue dragon.
My spiky tail isn't waggin'.

I need mead—pass the flagon,
'Cause I'm a blue blue dragon."

Grock looked scared as he took another step toward Bubbles. He was waist-deep in the moat now. He couldn't get much closer.

Suddenly, the horn playing stopped.

"Ah!" Bubbles shouted.

His eyes widened.

"Ah!" he shouted again.

His ears began to tremble.

"AH!" Bubbles shouted. Then he opened wide his jaws and out came: "AH-AH-AH-AH-CHOOOOOO!"

Wiglaf watched, amazed. It was as if all the air inside the dragon was expelled in that one huge sneeze. The sneeze sent Bubbles skimming backward on the water. And as he skimmed, he shrank down, down, down.

"Look!" cried Dudwin. "Bubbles is shrinking!"

"Fast!" said Bilge.

"Yeah," said Maggot.

Grock saw what was happening, and it made him bold. He splashed toward the shrinking dragon.

Bubbles kept shrinking until he was no bigger than a teacup. Suddenly, his bright blue eyes grew fixed and stared straight ahead. His wings seemed to melt into his back. His webbed feet stopped paddling. All that was left of the very dangerous Bubbles was a tiny blue dragon bobbing on top of the water.

Grock picked him up. "He be a goner!"

"Hooray for Grock!" all the Class I lads and lasses shouted.

"Hooray for Aggie!" shouted Wiglaf, and everyone clapped for her.

"Thank you," said Aggie, taking a bow. She turned to Wiglaf. "I don't need dragon slaying as a backup career. I'm transferring to a school for wandering minstrels!"

The Class II lads and lasses came running down to the moat now. Sir Mort, in full armor, appeared on the drawbridge. His visor was up.

"What's going on?" he muttered. "Where is Bubbles?"

Grock waded out of the water, proudly holding the little blue dragon as if it were a trophy.

"Now ye can call me Grock, the dragon slayer!" he cried.

"How did you do it, Grock?" asked Angus.

The troll shrugged.

"Tell us how!" said Janice.

"Come on, Grock!" said Erica.

"Yeah!" said Bilge and Maggot.

"Spill the beans, Grock," said Dudwin.

Sir Mort clanked over to them. "What's going on?"

Grock grinned. "Well, ye see," he said, "I waded into the moat toward the terrible beast..."

"Yes?" said Janice.

"And his snout starts going all quivery, don't it?" said Grock.

"Yes?" said Erica.

"I keeps wading, and gets closer and closer," said Grock.

"But how did you make the kill?" cried Erica.

Grock grinned and said. "I smelled him to death, didn't I?"

"You *what?*" cried Erica.

"Bubbles's secret weakness was sneezing," Wiglaf said. "When Grock gets scared, he smells like pepper. The pepper smell made Bubbles sneeze."

"That was the biggest sneeze I ever saw," said Dudwin. "But you don't smell like pepper now, Grock."

"That's 'cause I'm not scared no more," the troll said.

"Sir Mort is saved!" cried Angus.

"I am?" Sir Mort said. "That's good news!"

"And we owe it all to you, Grock," said Janice.

"Yah," said the troll. "Ye do."

All the DSA lads and lasses cheered for Grock. Wiglaf felt a little glow of pride for his Class I buddy.

"This here's for you, teacher," Grock said. He handed Sir Mort the tiny blue dragon.

"Why, thank you, lad," said Sir Mort. "Now I can take Duckie and Bubbles for little swims together."

Grock turned to Wiglaf. "Now gimme yer book."

Wiglaf slowly pulled *A Knight and His Dragon* from his belt.

"What are you doing, Wiggie?" asked Dudwin.

"I made a promise," said Wiglaf miserably.

What would Brother Dave say when he told him his precious book had been eaten? He held out the book to the troll.

Grock grabbed the book and put it up to his nose. He sniffed it eagerly. Then he licked the cover with his pointy, pink tongue. He started to drool.

Then he made a face.

"Don't you like it?" asked Wiglaf.

"Not good book, buddy," Grock said. "This old, stale book."

"It is?" said Wiglaf eagerly.

"YUCK!" said the troll, tossing the book back to Wiglaf.

"Thanks, Grock." Wiglaf smiled. The cover looked a little slimy, but the rest of the book was unharmed. Now he would find out what happened to the knight and his dragon, after all!

"Going home now," said the troll.

"What?" said Aggie.

"No, don't go!" said Dudwin.

"Don't!" said Maggot and Bilge.

"It won't be as much fun around here without you, Grock," said Dudwin. "Don't you like DSA?"

"Yah, I like," said Grock. "But I first troll dragon slayer," he added proudly. "I done here."

"Will you come and visit?" asked Dudwin.

"Sure," said the troll. "Promise." He turned to Wiglaf and waved. "Bye, buddy!" he said.

"Good-bye," said Wiglaf. He couldn't believe it—he was sorry to see Grock go. But he had a feeling he had not seen the last of the troll.